E   F   **Hoban, Russell**   83-58
HOB HOB
              Emmet Otter's jug-
              band Christmas

DATE			
6	12	7	
1	3	3	
17	M	10	2
Austin K K-I	10	4	
19	6	13	
1	SR	7	
3	3	JAN 0 5 2009	
Bri	JH		
6	gart		
MC	Port		
1	Port		
101	1		

© THE BAKER & TAYLOR CO.

EMMET OTTER'S JUG-BAND CHRISTMAS

PICTURES BY LILLIAN HOBAN ✳✳✳✳
✳✳✳✳✳ STORY BY RUSSELL HOBAN

Parents' Magazine Press / New York

83-58

Emmet Otter's Jug-Band Christmas

Christmas was coming and it was coming fast. It was
coming to the town where the houses huddled with their
cozy windows shining in the winter dusk. It was coming to
the country where the snow lay drifted up against the barns
and the firewood was all stacked beside the houses. And it
was coming to the river and the little run-down place where
Emmet Otter and his mother lived, near Frogtown Hollow.
Christmas was coming, and money was more scarce than ever.

Emmet Otter's father was dead, and his mother took in washing. There was no electricity out in Frogtown Hollow, and Mrs. Otter did her washing with a washboard and a washtub, all by hand. Emmet rowed up and down the river,

from Turtle Bend to Osprey Point, picking up the laundry that Ma's customers left on their boat landings, and he delivered it when it was done.

Emmet hauled the water and he did the chores. He cut the firewood and he stacked it. He went out with the tool chest Pa had left him, and he did odd jobs around the neighborhood. Every day he went out fishing. So there was always something on the table, and between the two of them Emmet and his mother paid the rent and scraped along somehow.

But it was always hard going, and this year was harder than ever. The crops hadn't been good; the sawmill down the river had been slow, and many animals were out of work. Housewives who used to give the wash to Mrs. Otter were doing it themselves. Grown animals, like Jake Beaver and Grover Muskrat who'd been laid off at the mill, were doing most of the odd jobs that Emmet used to get. "We'll get by somehow," Emmet and his mother used to say to each other. "We always have." But they were tired of just getting by.

"Last year I gave Emmet a muffler that I'd knitted," Mrs. Otter said to Irma Coon, "and the year before that it was mittens."

"Nothing wrong with mufflers and mittens, Alice," said Irma Coon. "It's the thought that counts."

"I know all about that," said Mrs. Otter. "But it's been such a rock-bottom life for so long, just once at least I'd like to bust out with a real glorious Christmas for Emmet—something shiny and expensive."

"It's a bad year for that," said Irma Coon.

"It's always a bad year," said Alice Otter, and she went on with her washing.

"Ma's never had it easy," Emmet said to Charlie Beaver. "We never had much even when Pa was alive, what with him being a traveling man, always up and down the river selling snake oil. He'd be gone for weeks on end sometimes, and when he did show up he never brought much money with him. Ma never complained, though. She said if Pa was willing to take a chance on snake oil she was willing to take a chance on him. I wish I could fix it so she didn't have to do any more washing, and if I can't do that, at least I'd like to give her one real good Christmas."

"There's no odd jobs this year," said Charlie. "I can't make a nickel, and my sisters aren't having any luck with Christmas cards or cookies either. Maybe it'll be a better Christmas next year."

"Some year it's got to be this year," said Emmet. "Last year I made Ma a sewing box, and the year before I carved a pie-crimper. Sometime she's got to have something fine and fancy that costs money, or I don't know what I'll do."

"Money's hard to come by," said Charlie, and he and Emmet both went off to do their chores.

When work was finished for the day, Emmet and his mother always went down the slide that Pa had built. In the summer they went off the end of the slide and into the river with a big splash. In the winter they slid down the slide and across the ice, whooping and laughing. But today they slid down quietly, both of them wondering what was to be done about Christmas.

In the evening they read aloud to each other by candle-light the way they always did, but neither one was paying attention to the book. Ma was thinking about a present for Emmet and Emmet was thinking about a present for Ma.

After they finished reading, Ma and Emmet sang together. They sang *Down the Slide with Dora, Swimming Nellie Home, The Bathing Suit That Grandma Otter Wore, We'll Go Fishing in the Moonlight,* and ended up with their favorite hymn, *Downstream Where the River Meets the Sea.*

Mrs. Otter had a lovely voice, and Emmet remembered her telling him that she had played the piano when she was a girl. Emmet wondered how many odd jobs it would take to buy Ma a piano, and he knew that he would probably never in his life be able to save up that much money. But the idea of a piano stayed in his mind and kept on growing.

Ma was thinking too. She was remembering how Emmet had looked at a beautiful secondhand guitar with mother-of-pearl inlays in a store window in town. Ma thought about how many washes it would take to buy that guitar for Emmet, and she tried to put it out of her mind, but she could not. Ma wanted Emmet to have that guitar for Christmas, and she didn't know what she could do about it.

Christmas was just two weeks off when Ma and Emmet heard some news that interested them both. Ma heard it from Hetty Muskrat, and Emmet heard it from Hetty's son Harvey.

"Fifty dollars cash," said Harvey. "How's that for a prize?"

"Prize for what?" said Emmet.

"The Merchants' Association is putting on a talent show in Waterville," said Harvey.

"What kind of talent?" Emmet asked.

"Anything," said Harvey. "Singing, dancing, playing instruments, reciting, acrobatics, juggling — anything at all. Have you got any talent?"

"I don't know," said Emmet. "Have you?"

"I've got a kazoo," said Harvey. "Wendell Coon knows how to blow a jug. Charlie Beaver has a cigar-box banjo. We could have what they call a jug band, maybe. We could call it the Frogtown Hollow Jug Band. All we need is a washtub bass."

"A washtub bass," said Emmet.

"That's right," said Harvey. "You set a washtub upside down, stand a broom handle up on the rim, and run a string from the top of the broom handle down through a little hole in the center of the tub. Then you strum it like a regular bass fiddle."

"A little hole in the center of the tub," said Emmet. "The trouble is, once you make a hole in the tub it won't hold water any more."

"Fifty dollars cash," said Harvey. "You could buy a lot of new washtubs with your share."

Emmet thought about it. If the Frogtown Hollow Jug Band won the prize, his share would be twelve dollars and fifty cents. With that he could buy a new washtub for a dollar and a half, put eleven dollars down on a secondhand piano, and pay out the rest. "When is the talent show?" he asked Harvey.

"Two days before Christmas," said Harvey.

"I'll think about it," said Emmet, and he walked slowly home.

While Harvey was telling Emmet about the talent show,
Harvey's mother was telling Emmet's mother. "I wish I had
some talent," Hetty Muskrat said. "We sure could use that
money."

"I guess we all could," Mrs. Otter said, wondering
whether there would be any really good singers in the show.

That night at dinner Ma and Emmet could hardly look each other in the eye. When they took turns reading, they kept losing the place in the book, and when they got around to singing *Downstream Where the River Meets the Sea* they both choked up a little.

The next morning at breakfast time the Otter house was empty. Ma's washtub was not in its regular place in the kitchen, and the broom was gone. Emmet's tool chest was not at the foot of the bed where he always kept it. There was a note on Emmet's pillow and there was a note on the kitchen table.

The note on Emmet's pillow said:

Dear Ma,
I have not run away. I will explain about the washtub and the broom when I see you Christmas Eve. There is plenty of frozen fish in the icebox.
Love,
Emmet

The note on the kitchen table said:

Dear Emmet,
I have not run away. I will explain about your tool chest when I see you Christmas Eve. There are clean underwear and shirts for you in your drawer.
Love,
Ma

That day, the few customers that Ma had left put out the laundry on their landings as they always did, but Emmet did not row by to pick it up. Upriver, past Osprey Point where the river branched off into swampland, was a little hut that Emmet and his friends had built there for a club-house. In the hut Wendell Coon was blowing his jug; Harvey Muskrat was playing his kazoo; Charlie Beaver was

picking his cigar-box banjo. And Emmet was strumming on his washtub bass and worrying.

Charlie Beaver was singing the words while he picked his banjo:

Going to Old Man Possum's shack—
Sister Possum waiting out back.

But Emmet was singing under his breath:

    Can't pay the rent if Ma can't scrub,

    Can't pay the rent with a hole in the tub.

"You better get with the beat, Emmet, if we're going to win," said Charlie.

Well, thought Emmet, if the Jug Band didn't win, maybe

he and Ma could go away someplace where things were better. As long as he had his tool chest, he could do odd jobs and they would get along somehow. But Ma wasn't going to have a piano unless they won. "Got to win," said Emmet, and he tried to keep his mind on *Sister Possum.*

While the Frogtown Hollow Jug Band was practicing up-river, Ma was downriver, at Esther Snapper's house in Waterville. She was sitting at her friend's sewing machine, making herself a dress to wear at the talent show.

"I don't quite understand this whole thing, Alice," said Esther. "You pawned Emmet's tool chest so you could buy that dress material?"

"That's right," said Ma. "And I'm going to sing in the talent show, and if I win the fifty dollars, Emmet's going to have that guitar with the mother-of-pearl inlays."

"But what if you don't win?" said Esther.

"I've still got my washtub," said Ma, "and we can always move on to someplace where things are better. They surely couldn't be much worse."

"I don't know," said Esther. "It sounds mighty chancy, but I certainly hope you win."

"Got to win," said Ma.

When the dress was finished, she practiced her songs and gestures in front of Esther's mirror and tried hard not to think of Emmet's tool chest that Pa had left him.

The night before Christmas Eve, the town hall in Waterville was all lit up for the talent show. There had been a lot of talk about it, and all the seats were taken long before the show was ready to begin.

Backstage the performers were getting ready to go on. The jugglers and acrobats were practicing their tricks; the musicians were tuning up; and the dancers were making last-minute adjustments on their costumes. Emmet was in

the men's dressing room and Ma was in the ladies'; so they
did not see each other.

Emmet and Wendell and Harvey and Charlie had been
practicing hard. They were going to play *Sister Possum*
first, and then *Downstream Blues* if they were asked for an
encore. Ma was ready, too, very stylish in her new dress.
She was going to sing *We'll Go Fishing in the Moonlight*
and *Swimming Nellie Home*.

Everybody in the Frogtown Hollow Jug Band was nervous. "We've got a good band," said Wendell Coon. "I know we sounded very good the last time we practiced."

"Sure we did," said Charlie Beaver.

"We'll win," said Harvey Muskrat.

"Got to win," said Emmet, and just as he said that, a whole lot of big cases on wheels rolled in with a whole lot of musicians following after.

"Who are you?" said Emmet.

One of the musicians, a woodchuck, pulled the cover off a set of drums. On the big drum was the name, *The Nightmare.*

"We're from River Bend," said the woodchuck. "Pete Squirrel and Jimmy Possum on the electric guitar; Herman 'Fats' Porcupine on electric bass; Jethro, Gideon, and Amos Mouse on electric organ; Henry 'Jellohead' Woodchuck —that's me—on drums; Mary Jane Chipmunk doing the vocals; and Fred Rabbit working the lights."

"We might as well go home," said Harvey Muskrat.

"Too late to back out now," said Emmet, and he tried to think of ways to plug the hole in the washtub. Then it was time for the talent show to begin.

Harrison Fox, the mayor of Waterville, thanked everyone who had helped to put on the show, asked the audience
to give everybody a big hand, wished them all a Merry
Christmas, and sat down.

The first act was Steve and Selma Rabbit, who tap-danced. Then Bascom Crow recited a tragic poem. Alfred and Deirdre Mole played short piano works for four hands. Bertha Toad and Winston Newt did a combination acrobatic and baton-twirling act. After each act the audience clapped a little and coughed a lot.

Then came the River Bend Nightmare, all of them wearing silvery, spangled costumes. They played a song called *Riverbottom Rock,* and while they played, the colored lights were making designs and patterns that jumped and shook and streaked like lightning on the walls and ceiling. The music roared and crashed and rattled windows all over town while Mary Jane Chipmunk moaned and hollered and screamed into the microphone.

When they were finished, the audience clapped and clapped for them to do an encore, and for their encore the River Bend Nightmare did *Swampland Stone*. The music roared and the lights flashed and the windows rattled again. And when the clapping finally died down, the silence filled the town hall like water filling up a boat with a big hole in the bottom.

Ma sang her song next, and it was like a whisper far away that nobody could hear.

Then came the Frogtown Hollow Jug Band, and when Emmet and Harvey and Wendell and Charlie played their music, it didn't seem to make any more of a sound than crickets and night peepers.

Then there were a few more acts. Somebody juggled and somebody else did magic tricks. Then the judges gave the fifty-dollar cash prize to the River Bend Nightmare. Then everybody wished everybody else a Merry Christmas and they all went home.

Ma and the Frogtown Hollow Jug Band were left by themselves standing in the street outside the town hall.

"Did you get my note?" said Ma to Emmet.

"No," said Emmet. "Did you get mine?"

"No," said Ma.

So they explained to each other about the washtub and the broom and the tool chest. Then they left the lights of the town behind them. They all went down to the river and started walking home on the ice.

"Well," said Ma, "we took a chance and we lost. That's how it goes."

"That's how it goes," said Emmet.

"It isn't going to be much of a Christmas for us this year," said Ma. "I was hoping to get you that guitar you liked."

"I was thinking of a piano for you," said Emmet.

"I guess I ought to feel pretty bad," said Ma, "but the funny thing is that I don't. I feel pretty good."

"So do I," said Emmet. "I don't know why, but I do."

Harvey Muskrat took his kazoo out of his pocket and began to play *Sister Possum* softly as they walked.

"That's a nice little tune," said Ma. "How do the words go?"

Charlie Beaver sang them for her, then Ma sang:

> Going to Old Man Possum's shack—
> Sister Possum waiting out back.

Then they all joined in the chorus:

> Rowing on the river,
> Rowing on the water,
> Going to dance the whole night long
> With Old Man Possum's daughter.

"Let's try it with the whole band playing," said Ma.

They were passing Doc Bullfrog's Riverside Rest and

stopped by the boat landing. Up above them in the lighted windows they could see everyone having a good time and they could hear the clatter of dishes, the tinkle of glasses, and the sound of laughter.

Harvey played his kazoo, Wendell blew his jug, Charlie picked his cigar-box banjo, Emmet strummed his bass and Ma sang as they all came on strong with *Sister Possum.* The music took off into the cold, clear air over the frozen river, and for a while they forgot the hard year they had had and the poor Christmas they could look forward to. Nobody noticed that the doors of the Riverside Rest had opened and Doc Bullfrog and his customers were listening.

"That's a mighty cheerful sound," said Doc Bullfrog as he came down to the boat landing. "That's a real down-home sound. What do you call your group?"

"Ma Otter and the Frogtown Hollow Boys," said Emmet.

"That's a good name too," said Doc Bullfrog. "How'd you like to play regular at the Riverside Rest?"

"Is the pay regular when you play regular?" said Emmet.

"It sure is," said Doc, "and your meals are on the house."

"What do you think, boys?" said Ma.

"We think we'd like that," said the boys.

"So would I," said Ma.

"Why not start tonight then?" said Doc Bullfrog. "After you have some dinner."

So they all went inside with Doc and had a good dinner. Then the band played and Ma sang until it was very late, and when they left for home they all had money in their pockets.

"Well," said Emmet to Ma, "it looks like I won't have to plug the hole in the washtub and I won't have to buy you a new one either."

"We've still got to have clean clothes to wear," said Ma. "What am I going to wash them in?"

"From now on we're going to send our laundry out," said Emmet.

Ma was quiet for a few moments; then she said, "I think I'd like to do a song for Pa, right here and now. He took a chance on snake oil and you took a chance on a washtub. He'd have been proud of us tonight."

So Ma Otter and the Frogtown Hollow Boys stopped there on the ice at three o'clock in the morning of Christmas Eve, and they did *Downstream Where the River Meets the Sea* for Pa.